THE
CLUB

Lisa Bahlinger (signature)

by Lisa Bahlinger
and Michael R. Strickland

for Caitlin
With Best Wishes!

Lisa (signature)

SUMMIT
BOOKS

Cover Illustration: Kay Salem

Dedication

To Revs. Timothy and Sharon Taylor—thank
you for your insight and help.

—L. B.

To Dr. G. Oliver Patterson—a special thanks.

—M. R. S.

Text ©2002 by **Perfection Learning® Corporation**.
All rights reserved. No part of this book may be
used or reproduced in any manner whatsoever
without written permission from the publisher.

For information, contact
Perfection Learning® Corporation
1000 North Second Avenue, P.O. Box 500
Logan, Iowa 51546-0500.
Phone: 800-831-4190 • Fax: 712-644-2392
www.perfectionlearning.com

Paperback ISBN 0-7891-5542-7
Cover Craft® ISBN 0-7569-0680-6
Printed in the U.S.A.

Lisa Bahlinger is a writer and freelance children's book editor. She earned a B.A. in English from Louisiana State University, and an M.F.A. in writing from Vermont College. She has received two fellowships to the Virginia Center for the Creative Arts. Lisa has written and published a number of poems and essays for adults and children, including several short essays in *African-American Writers: A Dictionary*, published by ABC-CLIO, 2000. She is a contributing editor to *The Other Side* magazine and is a member of the Society of Children's Books Writers and Illustrators. Lisa lives with her husband and daughters in Stone Mountain, Georgia. This is her first book.

Michael R. Strickland is a literacy educator, poet, anthologist, and historian who travels internationally speaking to children, teachers, and parents. Michael is a board member of the Maurice Robinson Fund, the Isaiah House Homeless Shelter in East Orange, New Jersey, and the Griffin-Bridges mentoring program at Seton Hall Preparatory School. He is a doctoral candidate in English Education at New York University, a graduate of Cornell University, and he earned a master's degree from Seton Hall University. His other books include *A to Z of African-American History*, *Poems That Sing to You*, *Haircuts at Sleepy Sam's*, and *African-American Writers: A Dictionary*. A fellow of the Institute for Arts and Humanities Education, Michael's workshops talk about using multicultural poetry across the curriculum and engaging readers and writers for balanced literacy.

ONE

TRUE'S heart pounded so hard he was sure anyone who walked by could hear it and would call the police. He reminded himself that no one could see him. He was invisible in the cold Philadelphia spring night, his coffee-colored skin and dark blue sweat suit blending in with the huge, old lilac bush in which he hid.

The lilac was in full bloom, and its heavy perfume made it hard for True to think. The smell of the flowers reminded him of when he had been a little boy on this street, before his dad left. It wasn't safe for little kids to play outside alone, even back then. He remembered how his dad used to walk along behind him as he rode on his brother's old bike with the training wheels. True used to love to pass by Mrs. Douglas's house when she sat outside on the steps or worked in her flower beds because she'd always look up to smile at him. "My, look at True!" she'd say. "He's coming up!" Or, "Could that be True? He's going to overtake his brother Wesley one of these days."

Then True thought of the time after his dad left them when his mom had been so sad and sick she didn't leave the couch. Mrs. Douglas watched him and Wesley after school for a whole week. Every day she gave them milk and store-bought chocolate cupcakes in plastic wrappers. And every day when she walked the boys home to their end of the block, she brought a little something for their mom like a Styrofoam container full of chicken soup, butterscotch disks, and a box of tissues.

But True didn't want to think about any of this. As he stood in the bush, shivering in the late-night air, True made himself think about the Club. He thought of Ringo and his posse. He imagined Ringo's face breaking into a rare smile as True brought him money and a VCR from Mrs. Douglas's house. True imagined Ringo giving him his very own Club jacket—the leather jacket he had been wanting for so long, the jacket that said you belonged somewhere, to someone.

Now True stared into the window of Mrs. Douglas's house and saw her as she passed by. She was wearing a pink robe, and her gray hair was all wrapped up in a white scarf above her golden brown, wrinkled face. True knew she was getting ready to go upstairs to bed because he'd been watching her house for weeks. True knew her neighbor in the duplex on the right, the old man, would be watching TV with the sound turned way up. True felt his heart beat and the sweat on his palms. He knew he didn't have to break into Mrs. Douglas's house. He could still change his mind. But when True pushed back through the heavy, wet lilac blossoms to the street, he saw Ringo and Allfire watching him from the corner lot, their plain white T-shirts bright as stop signs.

True knew he would do what he had come to do or Ringo and Allfire and the others would never want him in the Club. True took a deep breath. Then he took two strips of rags from his pocket and wrapped them around his fists. He picked up the broken brick he'd brought with him from the lot. True pushed the branches aside again to see that a light was still on downstairs, but it looked like Mrs. Douglas had gone up to bed.

True crept out of the bushes and slowly opened the rusty gate to Mrs. Douglas's narrow backyard. The gate squeaked in protest, and True froze to listen. He could hear car horns honking, doors slamming far off, people shouting blocks away. True walked quickly through the small, shadowy backyard. He climbed over the side of the back porch, over the railing. Without thinking anymore, he slammed the brick in his hand into the glass pane of the kitchen door, once, then twice. He heard it shatter. True reached through the jagged pane to unlock the door from the inside, then turned the knob. The door didn't open. Panicked, True felt all around the door until his hand felt a deadbolt high up on the frame. Something cut his hand, his arm, but he didn't notice. Sliding the deadbolt free, True opened the door.

Broken glass crunched under his feet. He could see through the small, dark kitchen to where an orange lamp glowed dimly from the living room. True didn't stop to listen now. He knew Mrs. Douglas might have heard the glass break. He darted into the front room and dumped out drawers from the coffee table, searching the room for money, a VCR, CD player—something, anything he could take back to the Club.

True didn't see Mrs. Douglas on the stairs, watching him from the shadows. So he didn't see her when she went back upstairs, quietly closed and locked her bedroom door, and called the police.

TWO

THE Youth Study Center, a juvenile detention facility, was shaped like a U. Even police cars had to pass through a gate with a guard into the open mouth of the U. In the middle was a sort of courtyard/parking lot. Calling it a courtyard made it sound nicer than it was. This was where everybody came in for admissions. Twelve years old or seventeen, shoplifting or murder, everyone passed through these doors and into the custody of the city of Philadelphia.

Later, True would remember walking in through those doors and knowing he'd try to run if he had the chance, but there was no chance. True would also remember how his heart sank as he passed into the building and how weak his knees felt because he didn't know what would happen next. And even years later, when he was asleep, he'd have clear dreams in which he remembered small details about the Youth Study Center, from the shape of an admissions officer's moustache to the color of the shoelaces of the boy beside him in the holding cell. (The shoelaces were red.)

That night, though, True didn't have time to think about anything. His knees and bottom lip hurt from being knocked to the sidewalk when a policeman tackled him from behind as he was coming out of Mrs. Douglas's kitchen. The next thing True knew, a man was leading him out of the police car and into a dark, dungeonlike room with no windows and locking him in "The Cage," a holding cell. True was now very scared. He didn't want to go into the cell, which was already full of mostly older black boys. Folding chairs lined the "walls" of the cell, which looked just how True thought they would—not solid but made of metal bars.

After a while, True and the other several boys brought in at about the same time, mostly teenagers ages 15–17, were told to line up. They were taken up one floor.

"Young man, put your clothes in this basket," the admissions officer said. He was an older man with creased, dark skin on his long forehead and skinny, wire-rimmed reading glasses on his nose. His closely cropped hair was the color of salt and pepper.

"My clothes?" squeaked True.

"Yes, son, your clothes. You get brought into the Youth Study Center, you don't get to keep showing out with your street clothes," said the older man, patiently. "Especially since showing out is most probably part of what brought you here in the first place."

The other admissions officer, a big, younger man with caramel-colored skin who'd been busy with some forms, turned and frowned. "Mr. James, don't call this young fool 'son.' *No* boy in here deserves to be called your son." The big man frowned at True, as if this kindness was somehow his fault.

True was exhausted and sweaty. It had been a long day, one he wished he could go back and do over. But what would he choose if he had to make the choice again? Not to break into Mrs. Douglas's house, or just to be more careful so he wouldn't get caught?

After True handed in his clothes, he was shocked to learn he was going to be body searched by one of the male guards. "To make sure you aren't hiding any illegal substances—that no drugs get brought into the Youth Study Center," said the guard.

It was humiliating, worse than visiting a doctor. After that, they were given their Youth Study Center clothes—heavy blue pants, underwear, T-shirts, socks, and tennis shoes with velcro straps. Everybody looked pretty much the same as they waited in line to see the nurse. True saw some showers in a nearby room and longed to take one, but nobody said anything about a shower. The nurse did a TB test, took blood, weighed True, took his temperature, and made him go into the bathroom with a paper cup for a urine sample. She spent some extra time with True examining his bottom lip, then his hand and arm, cleaning out the cuts and removing some tiny bits of glass. It hurt, but True was almost glad about this part, this gentle woman touching his arm, cleaning his wounds.

Then it was back past the tempting shower room with one dripping faucet and back down one floor to The Cage.

Back in the intake room, True flinched at the slam of the big metal door of The Cage. It was just like jail on TV, that part. There were so many people that chairs were lined up in The Cage as the kids waited to be sorted out.

Two of the teenagers were taken upstairs shortly after processing. When True asked where they were going, Mr. James said, "They are going to the fifth floor, and you best change your ways now so you don't end up on that floor."

True asked meekly, "What's on the fifth floor?"

"That's where the kids go if they kill somebody, or if they been brought in before for stuff."

True said, "What floor will I be sent to?" He was thinking of the tough, bored expressions on the faces of the teens who'd slouched out of The Cage when they were taken up to the fifth floor. True was relieved he was no longer sitting in the same room with them.

"How old are you?" asked Mr. James.

"Fifteen, sir," True managed to say.

"You'll stay right down here for now until we find you a placement. Just take a seat. If we can't find a placement tonight, you'll go upstairs like everybody else."

True tried to think. A placement? What was a placement? How long would they keep him here? What about his mom—would they let him call her or see her? And if they did, what could he say to her to explain where he was and what he'd done? The thought crossed his mind that maybe his mom would call his dad, and maybe his dad would come. He chased the thought away. Would he have to go to jail next? Why had he ever listened to Ringo?

True pressed his fingers to his eyes and tried

hard to block out The Cage, the sounds of the teenagers around him, and even his own thoughts. He tried to make his mind blank, like a fresh sheet of paper he could paint on. He wished he could start over. There was nothing he could do now to change what he had done. He would just have to wait to see what happened next.

THREE

WHAT happened next was that True sat on the folding metal chair for a long while, waiting. He watched as different people wearing plastic ID tag necklaces with their pictures on them came downstairs and took people out of The Cage, one by one. Mr. James explained that these people were social workers who worked at the Youth Study Center. True wondered what they did with the kids they took with them. Were they calling their parents, like at school? Were they locking the kids up somewhere else, by themselves?

A tall boy next to True, who looked like he was in his twenties, had just been brought in a little while ago and was still in his street clothes. After the first time some kids were taken out, this older boy turned to True and said, "What, they run out of men to pick on and they had to start bringin' in the little boys?" The teenager next to him, a stocky kid with a long face like a horse, snorted.

True slumped a little lower in his chair, trying to look tough.

"Ain't it past your bedtime, punk?" The mean kid said, trying again. He said it softly, like he was being nice. True felt nervous, but he was trapped in a jail cell with these people. What was he supposed to do?

True decided to get up and move to the other side of the cell, where there were now three empty chairs since some of the boys had gone up with social workers. Plus, Mr. James and Mr. Frown (the name True had given the strict, younger intake man) had desks closer to that side of the cell.

But when True stood up to move, he stumbled over the mean guy's outstretched shoes—FUBU shoes, $150 shoes, and before True had a chance to fall, the mean guy jumped up out of his chair. He caught True by the shirt collar, pulling him up, then slamming his back into the bars. True didn't have time to scream, but hitting the bars must have made some noise because the next thing he knew—as he hung there, eyes clenched shut, waiting to be smashed in the face—the next thing he knew, he had been dropped back onto a chair. Mr. Frown had the fighter in a neck hold. Mr. James pulled the teenager's hands behind his back and cuffed

16

him. Then they called security, and two guards came and took the fighter out of there.

"That's twice we saved your sorry self," Mr. Frown muttered to True, as he brushed the wrinkles out of his shirt with his hands. True noticed his name tag said, "S. Peterson."

"Twice?" True said, still clutching his collar. Nobody asked him if he was okay. Other kids in the cell just looked on, whistled, laughed, and talked to one another quietly. True's legs trembled as if he'd been for a ride on a roller coaster.

"Yeah, twice," Mr. Peterson answered. "Just now when I took that thug off your neck before he pounded you one—not that you don't deserve it, what you did to that old lady's place—and once pickin' you up and bringin' you in here. Before you have a chance to turn into somebody just as bad as that thug just now. Because that's just what's gonna happen if you keep makin' stupid choices, fool. You'll wind up here again. Only next time, might not be anybody to save your sorry self."

True stared at him.

"You understand what I'm saying to you?"

True shook his head. He was still shaking. Mr. Peterson sighed. "Look. One thing I've learned is you can run away from your problems for a while. Sometimes you can keep running for a long time. But sooner or later, you gotta make a choice. Are you gonna stand up for something? Is your life gonna stand for something? If it is, sooner or later you gotta stop running and face whatever it is that's coming at you."

True nodded miserably as the doors to the upstairs opened. A woman came in, wearing one of the plastic ID badges that meant *social worker* to True. She was tall and big-boned, with straight, shoulder-length hair and light, freckled brown skin. Her eyes looked sharp enough to see through you. She was wearing a gray suit and carried a clipboard on her hip. A pile of keys jangled on her wrist.

"Ah-ha, Sonia. I knew my evening was bound to get better. How are you tonight, dear?" said Mr. James.

"Fine, fine. Good to see you're managing to stay out of trouble. How's intake tonight? Looks busy," she said with a glance at The Cage, where some of the teenagers snickered at Mr. James calling her *dear*. Sonia glanced at her clipboard. I'm here to pick up True Monroe."

"Fine, Mrs. Lopez," said Mr. Peterson, keeping his eyes on The Cage.

True stood up and waited at the cell door. He could hear one of the boys, a raw-boned white kid with stiff orange hair, whispering under his breath about how he'd like to get picked up by Sonia too. True ignored it. He felt tired and stiff with an aching neck and back from getting knocked into the cell bars. And he was still sore where he'd gotten cut up on the broken glass. He was too tired to be afraid. He was glad that whatever was going to happen to him next would happen away from The Cage.

FOUR

SONIA Lopez took True out of the intake room and back up the stairs.

"My name is Mrs. Lopez," she said. "I'm your social worker. I tried to grab you earlier, but you were already with the nurse."

She took True down the hall. Though the walls were painted a pale blue, it was a sickly color, like the boy's bathroom at school, and True felt as if he were trapped in a nightmare. He thought he might be sick.

True noticed Mrs. Lopez's hair was streaked with red. She was wearing big, gold hoop earrings that swung as she walked. Mrs. Lopez turned left into a tiny, cramped room with peeling paint. There was a desk, a window with a metal grill over it, and two wooden chairs. Was this her office? It wasn't much nicer than The Cage.

"Have a seat, True," Mrs. Lopez said, waving her hand toward a chair. True was tired of sitting, but his stomach was still weak, and he sat down. "This your office?" he asked.

"Well, yes and no. I use it, but so do all the other social workers," said Mrs. Lopez. She began to ask True questions about himself, his family, friends, and school. She was interested in his father leaving, True could tell, because she started to ask a lot of questions about his mom. True didn't want to talk about his mother. Talking about her made True imagine her face when she was told by someone—a police officer? social worker? someone—that her son had been arrested by a police officer and locked up. The more True thought about his mom, the less True felt like telling Mrs. Lopez anything. How could he trust her? Whose side was she on, anyway?

"So, you might as well tell me about what happened tonight, True," Mrs. Lopez said, rubbing one of her earlobes where the heavy earring pulled on it.

"What happened?" True said vaguely.

"Yes, the break-in," said Mrs. Lopez patiently.

True was embarrassed. He didn't want to tell Mrs. Lopez anything, certainly not about the break-in. He glanced at her. She was studying him with those sharp eyes, but she didn't look angry, and she wasn't even frowning.

True noticed the way she jiggled her pencil between her thumb and finger. Didn't they teach people not to jiggle pencils in social worker school? thought True, who was feeling nervous already.

"Well, I did go into Mrs. Douglas's house . . ." began True slowly.

"Go in?"

"What?" said True.

"Go in? You didn't 'go in,' according to this police report. You broke a window to get in. That's breaking and entering."

True was starting to like Mrs. Lopez less. If she knew, why was she asking him?

"Okay. I broke in. I was looking for some money or a VCR or something."

"True," Mrs. Lopez continued, and True thought she said his name just like a teacher would when he wasn't getting something important, "what did you take from Mrs. Douglas's house?"

"Uh . . . not much."

"What were you carrying when the police caught you?" she asked, squinting down at her papers then back at True.

"Some tapes and stuff . . ." muttered True.

"Seven eight-track tapes, a macramé plant holder filled with coupons and greeting cards,

22

and $28 in bills and change," Mrs. Lopez read from the papers in front of her.

Now True was *sure* he didn't like Sonia Lopez. He could feel his face flushing. If she knew, why was she asking? Anyway, he hadn't meant to take those worthless eight tracks. Eight-track tapes! He didn't even know if they worked, they were so old.

But he had to take something back to Ringo! True remembered how he'd searched around, panicky, for something to steal. He remembered Mrs. Douglas's living room, how it was old-fashioned, wallpapered with yellow roses climbing up the walls. Decorated with lacy curtains that you could see right through and macramé plant holders hanging by the two windows with big green plants hanging down all around the windows. There were plants everywhere, in fact—pole-tall stalks with big leaves billowing out on top and flowering plants, like one with only a flower or two hovering over the leaves like pink butterflies. There were even some tiny trees that looked exactly like big desert trees, only about the size of a new pencil. True took in all this in less than a minute as he first stood looking around. No MP3 or DVD player, no VCR, no CD player. Just lots of plants and books.

But where was all the old lady's stuff? Here was a person who didn't have to go to school all day, thought True. If it were me, I would lay down some money for a really boss jam box with a CD player and a whole stack of music. You could jam all day—no one would tell you to turn it down.

Sure, the flowery wallpaper looked like what Mrs. Douglas would like, but instead of money or decent music, all True could find were those tapes, plants, and books, books, and more books. Why buy a TV cabinet if you don't have a TV? But that's what she'd done, and she'd filled it up with all kinds of plant stuff— pots, bags of dirt, and other weird stuff. True got mad. He started dumping stuff right out on the floor—eyeglasses, eyeglass cases, a mirror, notepads, pencils, and pens. Then he found a soft, red leather wallet with a zipper, full of quarters. He felt kind of bad then because it was the kind of thing an old lady would do, save quarters like that. He put it in his pocket, dumped a hanging plant from its macramé holder, and used the tightly woven basket-thing as a bag to stuff the eight tracks in. He didn't know. Maybe they were worth something; maybe they were antiques. They'd probably be worth a lot.

Then on his way out in the kitchen, True noticed a few streamers taped up and a small pile of cards lying on the kitchen counter. He took the cards too. Probably they had big, fat birthday checks in them—or better yet, crisp cash. True remembered with some embarrassment that what he saw that last minute had made him really happy. He saw a big gold ring lying on the windowsill, where Mrs. Douglas probably left it when she washed her supper dishes. He took that too, and stuck it in a tiny pocket in his T-shirt, underneath his sweatshirt. The ring was definitely worth some money. What True felt as he left Mrs. Douglas's house was not shame, it was pride. He felt really proud of himself, as if he'd really done something this time, something no one would forget.

But Mrs. Lopez hadn't asked about the ring. Was she just waiting to see if he'd admit taking it? Or was it possible no one knew about the ring yet?

FIVE

"**So** True, you took the neighbor-lady's mail?" asked Mrs. Lopez.

"I was looking for money. They were birthday cards. I thought . . ." said True, then he stopped.

"Money? What's all this about money? Money for what?" said Mrs. Lopez.

True didn't say anything.

"Money for drugs?" Mrs. Lopez asked him.

True looked up at her, surprised. "NO!" he shouted. Who'd told her that? What if his mom thought that too?

"Come on, True. Be straight with me. What did you want the money for?"

True thought. He didn't want to tell her anything about the Club or about Ringo. He said nothing.

"You think you're smart for not saying anything. Did those other boys have something to do with all this?"

"What other boys?" asked True, shocked.

This was the first time he'd heard that they knew anything about Ringo and the others.

"The other boys the police questioned tonight. You know them? Russell and William."

True was amazed. "NO! I mean, no, it's not about them. I mean, I don't know them. Except from school."

"Look, True. Like I said, you think you're smart for not telling me the truth about why you did what you did, but those boys are free, and you're the one sitting here, locked up with me asking you questions. So why are you protecting them?"

True was silent, angry.

"Something for you to think about, True—they didn't help you. They weren't good enough friends to want to get arrested with you. They let you come here for them. Are they really such good friends? You are acting tough for them—is that what you're going to tell your mom tomorrow when she comes in for your hearing?"

True's head was hurting. He was angry, hungry, dirty, and tired, and now he had the thought of his mom's face looking at him. And Wesley's. Then True imagined Ringo's sneering face. He'd let everybody down.

Mrs. Lopez continued. "Who is protecting your mom, True? Who's going to watch out for her?" True thought how Wesley would have to do everything, and how mad he would be with True for messing up like this. "This is no way to be a man, True," Wesley would say. Then he'd say, "When you gonna be a man?"

Mrs. Lopez jiggled her pencil and looked at her papers. True knew there was nowhere to go. He felt angry with Mrs. Lopez for talking like this about his friends and his mom, angry because she might be right, angry to think that one of these social workers could—and would— call his mom and tell her what he'd done. He thought of his mom, pictured her standing there a moment in her nightgown and slippers right after she hung up the phone. True wondered if his mom was worried about him now. Was she wondering where he was, or did she think he was upstairs, asleep in his own bed? Would the call from the Youth Study Center come as relief to her—at least they'd found him, and he was okay—or as a total embarrassment?

True was so upset thinking like this he couldn't stay there anymore. He got up, but he knew he couldn't run away. There were at least three locked doors between him and the parking lot, and someone was sure to catch him long before he got there. He looked at the window, but there was metal mesh over it. No way out.

Without really stopping to think, True punched the wall. He imagined Ringo's face as his fist made contact with the concrete. Then the pain blotted out everything.

SIX

THE nurse finished wrapping True's hand. True winced and flexed his fingers slowly. He'd taken the medicine they'd given him before they X-rayed his hand, and it was helping to dull his pain. All the anger had left True when he hit the wall. It seemed as if Mrs. Lopez would have been afraid of him after that. But she was not afraid, more like discouraged. Like she'd seen kids do stuff like this before.

The nurse mumbled to Mrs. Lopez as she worked on a bandage for True's hand. "Second time this kid's been in here tonight. Last time I thought he might need stitches for these cuts. Do you think you can keep him from breaking his neck?"

Mrs. Lopez flushed, and her lips pinched shut. She wasn't saying anything. True blushed too. He couldn't think of what to say either. What was there to say?

Since True had missed supper, Mrs. Lopez brought him an ugly plastic tray with little compartments from the cafeteria. There was salad, macaroni and cheese, green beans, and red Jell-O, with a little carton of milk. It was almost like school, except everything was upside down and wrong. True wasn't able to eat much. He kept thinking of everything that had happened, and his hand began to hurt and throb.

"Now that that's out of the way—and I want you to know you are really lucky you didn't break anything in that mass of bruises that used to be your hand—I want to talk with you a minute more," said Mrs. Lopez after she saw the nurse cleaning up her supplies.

"Okay," mumbled True.

"He's very lucky nothing is broken. It's going to hurt tomorrow, though," commented the nurse.

"That's out of the way now, right, True? The hitting? Because I want you to know it already cost you your placement tonight," said Mrs. Lopez.

"What do you mean?" True said.

"I mean I had a place lined up for you to go. A group home had agreed to keep you until your hearing with the judge. But after your little episode tonight with the wall, I had to call them back and tell them what you did to see if they still wanted you. And they didn't."

"They didn't want me?" True asked.

"No offense or anything, but people who go around punching walls aren't the most popular placements in group-home settings," said Mrs. Lopez sternly.

True didn't know why, but for some reason this really bothered him. He didn't want to go there to begin with, but how could they say they didn't want him? "Why can't I just go home?" True asked.

"Because you were picked up by the police for breaking and entering. You're going to have to sleep here tonight. Tomorrow we'll see, after your hearing with the judge."

True thought about the teenager who almost smashed him while they were locked in The Cage together. "Will I have to go upstairs?" True asked, eyeing Mrs. Lopez fearfully.

"Let's go see where there's a bed. Come on."

Mrs. Lopez walked True back down to The Cage. It was empty now. Mrs. Lopez called upstairs, and after a conversation with someone on the other end of the line, she hung up and turned to True. "There's a bed on the third floor you can sleep in. We are overcrowded tonight. There's not supposed to be more than one kid in a room, but for tonight you'll have to share. We'll see what we can do about a placement tomorrow."

"What about my hearing with the judge? When will that be?"

"I'll let you know sometime tomorrow when your hearing will be. Probably not until afternoon."

True was finally settled upstairs on a cot in a room with another kid who was already asleep. True didn't care if he had to sleep on a cot because he didn't want to feel at home there. But when he lay down on the creaky cot and waited for sleep to erase everything in his head, he found himself waking up instead. How had he ended up here? This wasn't supposed to happen. Why had he let Ringo talk him into this?

SEVEN

TRUE closed his eyes and thought back to meeting Ringo for the first time.

It was on a Friday afternoon. The school bells had already buzzed for the second time. Everyone had gotten up after the first bell ended the period, so the second bell was drowned out with people talking, banging locker doors, laughter in the halls, and shouts.

True bent over his bottom locker to put away his math book for the weekend. He knew he should take it home to study—he was barely passing math—but he didn't want to think about it over the weekend. Plus, what good would it do to bring his book home? His mother was no help with problems he didn't understand. She'd squint up her eyes and run her hand over her chin as she studied the problem. Then she'd sigh and say, "Sorry, Baby. I'm just no good with math." Or English. Or history.

True slammed his locker shut and looked up

to see Ringo, Allfire, and NoWay coming down the hall toward him. Allfire and NoWay were huge. True knew he was shorter than most boys his age were, but Allfire and NoWay looked like seniors, not sophomores. That is, until you saw them start pushing each other into trash cans and calling each other names. Ringo was not bulky like they were. He was lean, mean, and quick. Ringo liked to wear his hair in cornrows. Nobody laughed at him if he wore a hat or tried out some new fashion. Ringo was always styling, always cool, always loose.

True knew Ringo was the leader. He also knew their real names because teachers used them—Russell, Alfred, and José—but everyone, other than teachers, who made the mistake of calling them by their real names had gotten beat up. True tried to slip past them, but Allfire grabbed him roughly by his arm. NoWay just stood there with his pants hanging down around his hips and his boxers pulled way up.

"Yo, wait, we want a word with you, man," said Allfire. They'd never really spoken to him before. True stared down at the floor, trying not to look worried.

"What's up?" True said.

Ringo slapped Allfire on the head. "Not so rough with him, Allfire! You and NoWay go on home. I'll call you later." Allfire and NoWay looked at each other.

"You want us to go home?" asked NoWay. Ringo rolled his eyes in a friendly way at True.

"That's what I said, right? Later," said Ringo. Allfire and NoWay headed down the hall, looking a little lost without Ringo. NoWay had to keep pulling his pants up a little to keep them from falling down.

"So, True, right? That's your name?" said Ringo as they walked out of the now deserted hallway and across the parking lot.

"Yeah," said True.

"Sorry about Allfire grabbing you like that. See, Allfire got his name 'cause he always jumping to do something, you know? It's just like he was born on fire and he still burning."

"That's okay," said True. True was beginning to worry that Ringo was planning to beat him up or something. What was this all about? True kept hoping to see his friend William. They usually caught the bus together, but most everybody was gone already, and what was worse, it looked like True had missed the bus. True would have to catch a SEPTA bus. He'd be home late, and his mother would be mad. This was turning out to be a bad day, and he still didn't know what Ringo wanted with him.

"Hey man, I saw you put that senior straight yesterday in the cafeteria," said Ringo. "You were great."

"Oh, yeah? It was nothing." True said, looking away. True didn't know what Ringo was talking about. Then he remembered Wesley and his friends messing with him after his big test in geography yesterday. He was just pushing his tray down the line, and they were teasing him—tripping him, getting in his way, bumping his tray on purpose to try to make him drop it or fall. Finally, he'd lost his temper and shoved Wesley in the back. It wouldn't have been a big deal except Wesley was drinking chocolate milk at the time and started to choke, spraying milk all over the people in line ahead of him. Everybody was mad at Wesley for spitting milk on them and didn't know it was True's fault. Everyone except Wesley, of course, and now Ringo. True thought of telling Ringo that Wesley was just his brother, but he decided not to say anything. True liked Ringo thinking he was tough and wouldn't take teasing from anybody. What could it hurt if Ringo thought True was rough enough to take on a twelfth grader?

"What grade you in?" Ringo asked.

"Tenth."

"You're all right, man. Take it easy," Ringo said. He turned like he was going on home himself. True watched him go. A little way down the block, Ringo turned and called back, "HEY, TRUE—see you Monday."

After school Monday, Ringo met True by his locker again, this time with Allfire and NoWay. True missed his bus again. His mother wasn't there to notice what time True got home. She was probably at work at the hospital. The four of them walked to the corner WaWa, and Ringo bought subs, sodas, candy bars, chips, and cigarettes.

True couldn't believe it. He felt like anybody walking down the street could tell by looking at them that Ringo was too young to buy cigarettes, but nobody they passed even looked straight at them, much less said anything to them. True was also surprised by how much money Ringo had in his wallet. When Ringo paid for the snacks and cigarettes, True saw he had several twenties in his wallet. Where had Ringo gotten all the money? True was afraid to ask. But True enjoyed eating the chips and candy bars and drinking the soda.

"True, I bet you ten dollars you can't do a back flip," Ringo said when they got out into the parking lot of the WaWa.

True didn't know why Ringo would bet him that. "Right here? In the parking lot?" True said.

"Yeah, man. Right here, right now."

"No way, he can't do it," said NoWay. "He'll bust his head open."

True could do one, and he wanted the money because he was saving to buy a decent bike like Wesley's. So True put down his backpack and snacks and did a back flip right there in the parking lot. Ringo shook his head and acted surprised, but True thought he was pleased.

Ringo handed True a ten-dollar bill. True couldn't believe it. What an easy way to make ten bucks!

"Just listen to me, True. If you do like I tell you to do, I'll see to it you always have enough money to buy what you want," Ringo said. "I promise."

"No doubt," said NoWay, with a sneer.

EIGHT

REMEMBERING that day, True thought about Ringo's promise. He hadn't promised to be his friend. He hadn't promised to stand up for him. Ringo'd said *if you do what I tell you to do, I'll pay you.* True hadn't thought much about that at the time. Now he wondered if that was what a friend would say to you.

True remembered how he'd started meeting Ringo after school everyday. Sometimes Allfire and NoWay were there too, and sometimes they weren't. When they weren't there, if True asked about them, Ringo might say, "Pay them no mind," or "NoWay who?"

One day after school, Ringo said, "True, come on up to my apartment, and I'll give you twenty dollars."

True looked at him. "What for?" True asked.

Ringo laughed. "What do you mean, what for? Man. I just want you to take something to a friend of mine."

True didn't know whether Ringo was just

messing around with him or if he was telling the truth, but he really wanted the twenty dollars if Ringo was serious.

"Straight up? Why can't you take it yourself?" True asked.

"Oh, I would, True, but I got someplace to be. You know I haven't asked you for nothing. Who's always taking care of you, anyway? Buying you stuff?" Ringo said, his voice getting angry. He flipped up the stiff collar on his leather jacket. "Man!" he said, "Some friend!"

"Okay, okay, Ringo. I'm sorry. It's just I've got to hurry up. My mom's expecting me at home," True said. Then he was sorry he'd said anything about his mother.

"No doubt, your momma's missing you! No doubt!" said NoWay. Allfire smirked and raised his eyebrows at True. True could feel himself getting hot in the face.

"Later," said Ringo to Allfire and NoWay as he left school with True.

Ringo lived in Paradise Towers, the high-rise, low-income apartments on Pulaski. Nobody knew why it was called Paradise. There were no rivers or parks in sight, not parks with swings and ball fields, anyway. Germantown had been a quiet suburb of Philadelphia a long, long time ago, with brick-lined avenues, huge trees shading a few wide boulevards, big stone homes, and several parks full of babies in strollers. Before that, before the neighborhood was there, Germantown itself was like one big park. Rich people from Philadelphia used to ride out to the countryside, to Germantown, to escape the heat of the city. Philadelphia grew up and around Germantown, and it was now part of the city. There were some empty, overgrown, trash-strewn lots with a few benches, but homeless people now claimed them.

People who lived in Paradise Towers called it Vice. Some called it that because of the trouble that some people caused there; others called it that because it was the kind of place that seemed to catch and hold people, like in a vise. Tight. *No escape*, somebody spray painted over the words *fire escape*.

Nobody knew why it was called *towers* instead of just *tower*. Maybe the plan back in 1970 when the thing was built had been to build two or three of them. If so, the plan fell through, and just one tall building stood on the street, eight stories tall. The stairways were all on the outside of the building, covered in wire mesh. They were outside, so people could see most of what was going on in the stairways, even from the ground, but the mesh was to keep people from falling or getting pushed off.

True knew he wasn't allowed to be there. His mother would be furious with him if she ever found out. She had always been nervous about living so close to Paradise and told Wesley and True not to go there. As far as True knew, Wesley never did.

Wesley was too busy fooling with his Trek bike, tuning it up with tiny wrenches or taking it out somewhere for a spin. Wesley loved his bike. He had saved all the money he made last summer as a day-camp assistant counselor to buy his bike, a Trek Alpha SL 2200 racing bike. It was electric yellow and blue. The bike was fast. It was so fast, even when it was hanging from ceiling hooks in True and Wesley's bedroom, the bike appeared to be flying.

True could almost believe it was a magic bike because of what it did for Wesley. On his own, Wesley was shy and quiet, and he wore wire glasses with thick lenses. He liked to read about navy fighter planes, and then he liked to build them. Wesley had a WWII Grumman F6F Hellcat and an F-14 Tomcat hanging on fishing line from the ceiling of their room too. But when Wesley got on his bike and fastened his helmet under his chin, he suddenly looked much older. Wesley would take off down Schoolhouse Lane, avoiding the bumpy, old brick of Germantown Avenue. Though he was a careful biker, he seemed to float through traffic and up toward Mt. Airy and Chestnut Hill, or down Lincoln Drive to Kelly Drive to wind along the Schuylkill River. Down by the river, Wesley blended in with the steady stream of other cyclists, joggers, and in-line skaters who enjoyed the beautiful view of people rowing along on the Schuylkill by Boathouse Row.

True knew his mom worried about the drug dealers at Paradise Towers, and that's why she didn't want True or Wesley to go there. But he felt safer being there with Ringo, and True told himself it wouldn't matter just this once. As he climbed up the stairs behind Ringo, he wondered to himself why the building was named Paradise. It's like the projects, thought True, only the people who live here are stacked up on top of one another. Why does Ringo live here with his family if they have so much money they can give Ringo enough allowance to buy snacks for everyone every day?

True felt a little sick to his stomach as he walked up. Graffiti was spray painted all over the inside walls of the building. Even though the stairs were open, the staircase smelled like cat urine and fried fish at the same time. There were candy wrappers, empty beer bottles, and somebody's newspapers now matted and shredded against the wire mesh. True kept his hands in his pockets. He didn't want to touch anything. Ringo didn't seem to notice. He seemed relaxed and happy True was with him. He kept talking about how long he'd lived there, how they'd move soon now that his dad had a job. When Ringo unlocked his door on the fifth floor, he stopped after he stepped inside. True could just make out the shape of a man lying there, sound asleep on the couch in the dark room. There was a blanket hanging over the window, but a TV in the corner was on, and by the flickering light of a game show, True could see some empty bottles on the floor.

"Stay here," Ringo muttered to True. He pushed the door closed, leaving True outside. True was nervous. Was that Ringo's dad? What had happened to him? Wasn't he supposed to be at his new job? In a minute, Ringo stepped back out and quietly closed the door behind him. He looked at True with a cold, hard stare.

"You didn't see that," he said. In his hand he held a small manila envelope. He slipped the envelope into True's hand. The envelope was surprisingly light. "Take it to the barbershop down at the corner of Pulaski and Wayne. There

45

will be a guy waiting outside, a tall dude with a gray cap he wears backward. Tell him, 'It's True,' and if he says, 'It's not,' you can give it to him," Ringo said. "He'll give you something to bring back to me."

True nodded slowly.

"Don't let me down now, True," said Ringo.

True stuffed the envelope into his backpack. He could feel some lumps in the bottom of the envelope. He wanted to ask Ringo what it was, but he could tell Ringo was in no mood to tell him anything. True guessed Ringo's mind was probably on the man sleeping in the apartment.

True could feel Ringo watching him as he went down the stairs alone and back out onto the street. He didn't feel safe anymore now that he was alone. He felt as if there were a sign on his head that said "up to no good." He didn't like the uneasy feeling he had, knowing that whatever he was carrying was probably not something that belonged to Ringo. What was it?

True wanted to know what was in the envelope. At the corner store next to a bar where some men were hanging around, True looked back over his shoulder. Ringo was no longer watching. True took the envelope to the empty lot on his block. He dragged an old tire to sit on behind a mattress leaning up against the wall.

He carefully unstuck the flap on the envelope, trying hard not to tear it. It only tore a little. Then he turned it upside down and shook out some small wads of tissue. Inside the tissues, True found a pair of diamond earrings, a diamond necklace, and a gold pocket watch.

Who did the jewelry belong to? It must have been stolen. True felt sick inside as he stuck the jewelry back into the envelope and stuck the flap closed. He wished he hadn't looked. He didn't know where the jewelry had come from, but he wanted to get rid of it. True thought of what would happen if he were caught with it, especially if it had been stolen from someone. No wonder Ringo had asked True to deliver it. He wanted True to take the risk of getting caught. If he needed it, here it was—proof that Ringo couldn't be trusted.

True took the envelope to the barbershop and saw the man waiting outside like Ringo had said he would be.

"It's True."

"It's not," the man mumbled, then stuck out his hand and took the envelope True offered to him. He then took a crumpled regular envelope from his back pocket and handed it to True before walking off down the street without another word.

47

When True walked back up the staircase, it felt like the wire mesh was closing in on him. True wanted out of there as soon as he could. He started to knock on Ringo's door, but Ringo answered right away, like he was waiting for him.

Ringo said, "Well?" and held out his hand. True gave him the envelope, then turned to go.

"Wait! Here's your twenty bucks," said Ringo, holding out a bill.

True didn't want the money anymore. But he took it, crumpled it up, and shoved it in his jacket. Then he hurried away down the stairs as fast as he could go.

About six weeks after True had started missing his afternoon bus on purpose to hang out with Ringo, True came in, and his mom was there waiting for him. True was surprised. Mostly his mom was not at home. Usually she was at the Veteran's Hospital where she worked part-time as an aide, or out paying bills, or grocery shopping. When she was home, she was usually in bed. Some days she never got dressed. Some days it was like a huge cloud had her shoulders pinned to the bed.

True had learned to start taking *weather reports*, and he and Wesley would relay them to each other. *Weather report, September 7th—cloudy with a chance of thunderstorms* would mean, "Mom is in bed and may be crying soon."

That day, however, she was not only up, she was looking good. Forty years old, True's mother had her dark brown hair smoothed straight back in a twist. The royal blue blouse she was wearing set off her medium brown skin. She was wearing a matching skirt and high heels. And she was wearing a frown on her face.

"Aren't you late getting home, son?" she said to True.

True was surprised she'd even noticed. She hadn't said anything before. "The bus schedule changed. I have to ride the second load, so I just get back later now," True lied. "Why are you all dressed up, Mom?"

"I had an appointment. I'm going to work on getting back into nursing. Being an aide is blue-collar work and just don't pay," True's mom said. "I had to meet with someone in admissions up at the Community College to see what I need to do."

"Nursing?" True said, glad they weren't talking about his schedule anymore.

"We just can't get by forever on savings and money from your grandma. I have to get a full-time job again."

True remembered feeling surprised at how easy it was to lie to his mom about where he'd been. But he told himself that she wouldn't like him hanging around with Ringo, and he didn't want to stop. He liked the way the kids at school who had ignored him before now paid attention when he walked by with Ringo, Allfire, and NoWay, even if they looked afraid of them. He liked the free soda, chips, and candy that Ringo bought. So he ignored the little questions that rose up in him like soda bubbles. *Why doesn't Ringo like to answer your questions? Why are other kids scared of him? Why does Ringo want to be friends with you, True?* And, even harder, *why do you want to be friends with him?*

"I'm sorry, Mom," True said out loud into the stale air of the Youth Study Center room, thinking of all the lies he had told his mom. He felt like he'd never been so far away from home or so unsure of what tomorrow would bring.

NINE

WHEN True woke up the next morning, all he knew at first was how sore he was all over, but especially his arm and hand. When he sat up and saw the bandages, he remembered everything that had happened the day before. The hearing was today. All True could think about was seeing his mother. He dreaded that awful look he knew he'd see on her face at first. It would be a look of disappointment in him. It was the look she had worn for months after True and Wesley's father left them. Hadn't True disappointed her too? But then, after the hurt look, True hoped his mother would lean in and hug him. Of course, he would never have admitted this to anyone. But it had been a long time since his mom had hugged him, and he wanted so much for his mother to be his *mother*—to take care of him, to help him get out of the Youth Study Center forever.

It wasn't quite like True thought it would be. Why wasn't it ever like he thought? Why wasn't his mother the kind of mother he thought she should be?

The morning flew by. True dressed when he was told to and ate breakfast with the other boys on his floor when they were called. He went to the bathroom when he was told to, made up his cot, and waited for Mrs. Lopez. Before he knew it, Mrs. Lopez came for him to take him downstairs to the lobby of the Youth Study Center and wait for the hearing.

True sat on a metal folding chair next to Mrs. Lopez, who absentmindedly flipped her pen between her finger and thumb again and read over some papers from the pile of files on her lap. There were about 30 chairs in the lobby, with several people waiting there to meet family members. On the right side of the large front door as you walked in was a counter, which was a security desk with two security guards behind it to check in the visitors after they walked through the metal detectors.

A large staircase came down from a second-story landing, and you could see the two men in suits standing up there looking down. True and Mrs. Lopez were outside of the tiny courtroom on the left side of the main lobby, waiting their turn with the judge.

"Are those papers all about me?" True

asked. Mrs. Lopez laughed.

"No, True, you aren't my only case. I have more than 50 other kids right now. A lighter load than I sometimes have."

This seemed like a lot to True. How could Mrs. Lopez help him if she had that many other people to keep track of?

Just then True saw his mother coming up the stairs toward the front door of the building. He saw her before she spotted him. She was dressed in a yellow dress with a collar open at her neck and buttons all down the front. And she was even wearing pantyhose and high heels! True could remember the last time she'd looked this good. It was the day he'd lied to her about his bus.

Now here she was, her hair pulled back in a clip. She looked older, stubborn, and a little sad. She had not seen him right away. True slid down in his chair without realizing he was doing it.

True tried to imagine what he would think of his mother if he didn't know her, if she were someone else's mother. She looked okay, not mean, not too old or too young. But still True felt embarrassed by seeing her there, as if she were the one in trouble. After she signed in with the guards, she saw True and Mrs. Lopez and made her way across the lobby to their side.

"True," she said, but when True looked up, Mrs. Lopez stood, shook his mother's hand, and introduced herself.

"Nice to meet you, Ms. Monroe. I'm Sonia Lopez, True's social worker," said Mrs. Lopez.

"It's a pleasure to meet you," True's mother said with a quick smile before she looked down.

Mrs. Lopez began to talk with True's mom in a chatty sort of way, like two strangers who start a conversation in the grocery store. True was surprised to see her there smiling and speaking in a low voice to his mother, saying something True couldn't hear. They looked so calmly at each other—Mrs. Lopez there in her thick wool suit that reminded True of shredded wheat cereal and his mom in yellow, more dressed up than she'd been in months. True knew it was all because of him, because she had to be there, because of what he'd done to Mrs. Douglas's house. True tried to imagine his mom all dressed up like this, only proud of him, at his graduation from high school or college. She would take pictures at a time like that. But not here, not now.

Mrs. Lopez and True's mom kept talking— was it about him?—as though he weren't there. True felt angry and embarrassed by this. He felt like he had when he was a little kid and in some kind of trouble for not sitting still in school. Then the teachers would make him sit by the door in the time-out chair while they talked about him right over his head, saying things like, hadn't he had enough sleep last night, had he mentioned skipping breakfast, and it just wasn't like him.

True knew this wasn't the same; this was much, much worse. For a moment Mrs. Douglas's soft, wrinkled face flashed to his mind. True realized he hadn't asked Mrs. Lopez if Mrs. Douglas was okay. Not that he'd taken much, but if she was okay, if she'd gotten the glass cleaned up. If she'd stopped being mad at him. True thought he'd have time, a few minutes, anyway, to talk with his mom before the hearing. But before True could think of how to ask about Mrs. Douglas, his name was called, and it was almost time to go into the small courtroom.

Mrs. Lopez told them she needed to quickly explain today's proceeding to them. This was a detention hearing, not a trial. The judge was not going to decide if True was innocent or guilty today. Today's hearing was just to decide where True would live while he waited for his judiciary hearing. He might be sent to a group home, a community-based shelter, or maybe home to be supervised by his mom. The judicatory hearing in a few weeks was to determine True's guilt or innocence. Then there would be a third hearing, called a sentencing hearing, where the judge would tell him his punishment if he was found guilty. Mrs. Lopez said that today the judge would want to talk with True and his mother to see if they understood the seriousness of the charges and if True's mom could handle watching over True until the judiciary hearing.

True was upset to hear he had two more visits with the judge after this one, but there was no time to think about it now. As True sat down in the courtroom, he wondered if the judge would keep him here, locked up with people he didn't know. What would happen next? Would he sleep in his own bed tonight, or was he going to be sent somewhere else?

TEN

THE small, windowless room didn't really feel like a courtroom to True. It didn't look the way he thought it would, anyway—the walls were not wood-paneled the way they were on TV shows, there was no jury and no long rows of wooden benches like church pews or tall windows to stare through for a long look at the outside world. Instead, True found himself in a room not much bigger than a principal's office with a few rows of metal folding chairs that faced in the direction of the judge's desk. The judge's desk was on a platform behind a railing, and there was a little desk for the court recorder to sit and take notes. Mrs. Lopez, True, and Ms. Monroe sat down up front. True's mom sat by him, but he noticed she hardly looked at him. She seemed afraid, as if she were on trial.

Judge Caroset was presiding. He was already seated, looking over papers. He wasted no time, beginning immediately after they sat down. He nodded to Mrs. Lopez and asked her to begin. It wasn't the same at all as going to criminal court. Mrs. Lopez told Judge Caroset what the charges were, that True had never been arrested before, and that she thought while the charges were serious, True would do best in home detention until the judiciary hearing.

"Although," the judge said, "there was the incident of hitting the wall. We'd need to be sure he isn't dangerous to other people." He glanced at True.

True looked at his shoes. Why'd he hit the stupid wall? What a dumb thing to do.

Mrs. Lopez said while she didn't approve of what he'd done, he hadn't tried to hurt her, and he hadn't struggled with the arresting police officer. The judge then spoke to True's mother, asking her to tell him what she thought about whether True could be trusted to obey the rules of home detention if he were sent home with her. True watched his mother stand and slowly smooth the wrinkles on her dress. She looked very embarrassed. True was sure she was furious with him, but when she spoke, she sounded more sad than angry.

"Your honor, True's always been a good boy. I've had to raise True and his brother Wesley without any help—that is, on my own since their daddy and I divorced. I never planned on being a single mom, and I know it's been real hard on them. There have been times when I was sick that I didn't do everything I should have to make sure they were okay. I regret that very much . . ."

Ms. Monroe paused, and True thought to his horror she might cry. *Weather report—storm at court . . . film at eleven.*

Judge Caroset gave Ms. Monroe a moment, then asked her what she meant by *sick*.

True's mother continued, explaining that after her husband left, she was depressed for a long time. "But," she said, "I'm better now, and I'm looking for a better job. I want to be a better mother to Wesley and True. I'll do whatever the court tells me needs to be done to help my son get his life straightened out again."

True didn't look at his mom. He wondered if she meant what she was saying or if she was just saying it to try to fool the judge. Was she really looking for a better job? Did she mean what she said about him being good? Did she really believe in him?

While his mother spoke in her slow, careful way, True looked at the judge. Judge Caroset was a middle-aged white man with wire-rimmed glasses shadowing his sharp blue eyes. He had a very peaceful attitude and appeared to be listening so hard he may have been listening for something going on in the next room for all True knew. He listened to True's mother with his elbows resting on the desk in front of him, his fingertips just touching.

When Ms. Monroe finished and sat down, Mrs. Lopez patted her on the arm a few times, then waited for the judge to speak. Judge Caroset closed his eyes and looked like a monk at prayer. True didn't know if it was a good or bad sign to have a judge fall asleep while you were in his courtroom, but he thought it could be a bad sign. Judge Caroset wasn't asleep, however. He began to ask True's mom some questions. What has your family life been like? How long has it been since your divorce? Tell me about your work history. Who watches over True after school? What about your other son? How is he doing in school? Is he staying out of trouble?

After Ms. Monroe answered these questions, Judge Caroset told her if he allowed True to go home, he would have strict rules about what he was allowed and not allowed to do. He would go to school as usual, but he'd have to come straight home. He wouldn't be allowed to go to friends' houses, to after-school activities, or to work an after-school job. He would have home visits from a court-appointed social worker.

"True requires adult supervision at all times." Did Ms. Monroe know what that meant? He was in serious trouble. Was she going to be able to guide him? True's mother began to look angry and maybe a little afraid, but her face was determined. Yes, she understood the responsibility of home detention, and she would supervise True until the judicatory hearing if the court allowed her to.

Judge Caroset didn't seem as sure. He looked sternly at Ms. Monroe and at True. He said, "I see dozens of young people in this courtroom, and I have heard a lot of promises." He removed his glasses, held them to the light, and seemed to make up his mind. He said again that True was not to be left unsupervised. He was placing True in home detention under his mother's supervision, and he would see True again in ten days for his judicatory hearing.

True was relieved and happy. It felt as if he were free, even if it was just temporary, even if this was just the first hearing and not the last.

ELEVEN

OUTSIDE the courtroom, Mrs. Lopez said, "Well, that's good. Now Judge Caroset said he'd see you in ten days for your next hearing, but the judiciary hearing probably won't happen that fast. It usually takes longer than that to get all the paperwork ready. In the meantime, the good news is you get to go home with your mom. Someone will be assigned to come by your house to check on you every day until your next hearing."

Mrs. Lopez turned to True's mom. "True needs to go to school, and that's all. He's lucky the judge isn't sending him to a shelter." Then she said to True, "You need to make sure to follow the rules of the home detention. If you get picked up again for something else, the judge won't send you home again. You got that?"

True nodded. Then the three of them went back to admissions where True was given his own clothes to change back into. He was glad to take off the Youth Study Center uniform, but it was uncomfortable to pull the dirty T-shirt and sweat suit back on.

When True pulled his T-shirt on over his head, he remembered Mrs. Douglas's gold ring. Had the admissions officers found it? Mrs. Lopez hadn't mentioned it in the questions she had asked him during the admissions interview. True carefully checked the tiny pocket of the sleeve—and sure enough, the heavy gold band was still there. True thought about it as he pulled on his sweatshirt and shoes. What should he do with it? Should he keep it? Give it to Mrs. Lopez or to his mom? He didn't know. True decided to wait to tell them about it. Maybe after he was back at home, he'd be able to think more clearly. Right now though, he just wanted to get out of here and forget everything that had happened in the last couple days.

True's mother, however, did not plan to let True forget what had happened. As they walked out into the late afternoon, True took deep breaths of the fresh spring air. Traffic was heavy, as usual, on Ben Franklin Parkway, as people zoomed by the Youth Study Center on their way toward the art museum and away from downtown. True was amazed to see people going about their ordinary lives.

"What day is today?" True asked his mom.

"Today is Thursday," she mumbled, unlocking the door to her old blue Geo Metro. She'd parked by a meter down the street from the Youth Study Center. True found it hard to believe it was just Thursday. It seemed to him like he'd been gone for a very long time. He was happy to see the gray sky. The sidewalks and street were still wet from a heavy rain; a few battered-looking daffodils were blooming in mud. True was glad to see them, glad to get into his mother's old car for once. Usually he complained and was embarrassed to ride in it, but not today.

In fact, True felt so good, so glad to be out, he almost believed it was a holiday. "Where to, Mom?" he said as he climbed in, slammed the door, and fished around for his seatbelt. "Can we go out to eat? I'm starved."

If True thought his mother was going to feel sorry for him and take him out to eat, he was wrong. She looked at him for a moment as if she'd never seen him before.

"True, you are under home detention. Didn't you hear a word the judge or Mrs. Lopez said? Did you think they were just talking *at* you? Flapping their mouths just for the fun of it? Wise up, True! They were talking to *you*. We are not going out to eat. We have nothing to celebrate. Wesley's expecting us at home, and in case you were wondering, we've been worried sick about you."

With that, she cranked the engine, shifted into first, and eased off the parking brake and the clutch. True tried for the umpteenth time to roll the window all the way up. But, as usual, there was still a one-inch gap at the top, and the window refused to roll up any higher. True was cold. March in Philadelphia, and True didn't even have a jacket on. The Geo Metro was a car his mom had bought used after seeing it in a newspaper ad. The car had over 100,000 miles on it and was only five years old. True sighed, his happy mood gone. Here he was, finally free, and he was freezing, hungry, and wishing he were someone else.

As True's mother merged into the traffic, she seemed to have very little to say, and True thought it was like she was done talking to him. Period. But he was wrong again. As they turned onto their street, his mom glanced over at him and said, "Things are going to be different around here from now on. I know I haven't been there for you the way I thought I always would, the way I'd like. And that's going to get better. We are a family, True. I can't make your daddy come back home. But you belong here with us, not out running the streets with kids who don't know right from wrong, and not locked up in some juvenile prison. But you are going to have to make some changes too, son. You are going to have to stay away from trouble."

True didn't know what to say. He couldn't remember his mom talking this way before. But those words his mom said, about being in a family and belonging, stirred his heart and made him want to believe her. They made him want to be strong, like a man, for her. He would do better. He would try to stay away from the Club and everyone in it when he went back to school. Right now, he didn't even want to think about them. What he wanted most was a shower, followed by hot food and his own soft bed.

TWELVE

TRUE dressed for school in jeans, a T-shirt, and a pullover, then pulled on his jacket. His bandaged right hand hurt and made even simple things hard to do. He pushed his left hand deep into his jeans pocket to hide the nagging weight of Mrs. Douglas's gold ring. Maybe he should give it to his mom today. True slowly laced his basketball shoes, the cheap Payless basketball shoes Allfire and NoWay liked to laugh at, calling them BoBos. True thought of the FUBU basketball shoes he could buy if he stayed in the Club and kept saving his money. He imagined NoWay admiring the new shoes, *"Truue. Swweeeeet."* He had almost enough to buy the shoes now, but he still wanted a bike like Wesley's too.

True's mom was up and dressed before her sons. "Remember what we talked about, True," she said as True said good-bye to her. True remembered. She wanted him to stay away from trouble. He would, he promised. But it couldn't hurt just to sit with William on the bus. William wasn't actually in the Club any more than True, even if Ringo had nicknamed him "Boy," which fit because William looked no more than 12, even though he was 15 too.

True walked out to wait for his bus. He tried not to look at Mrs. Douglas's house as he walked toward it, but he couldn't help it. True's mom had given him a big lecture about violating someone like Mrs. Douglas, someone who had taken care of him through the years. True knew it was wrong. He didn't want to be reminded of it again, but his eyes seemed drawn to the house.

As True looked up, he saw Mrs. Douglas's neighbor, the old man. The old man came down his front steps, wrapped in a large black overcoat. He waited for True to come closer. Oh, no, thought True. He's going to yell at me. Well, maybe he doesn't know who I am.

"Home already, are you?" said the old man. Now that he was close to him, True could see the old man's ashen face was deep brown, his head nearly hairless, but he had big, feathery eyebrows like fuzzy caterpillars.

"Sir?" said True.

"Back home from wherever the police took you? They may not be able to hold a young person like you for long, but I sincerely hope you learned a lesson." The old man paused to cough something up, then rubbed his hands together as though he were enjoying this.

True searched down the small street for his bus, but it wasn't coming yet. He looked back toward his house at the other end of the street, but Wesley wasn't coming yet, either. True shoved his left hand into his pocket, accidentally touching the ring.

"Uh, mister, I don't even know your name. I probably shouldn't even be talking to you," True said.

"Is that a fact? You can steal from folks you do know, but you ain't allowed to speak to strangers. Well, I like that," said the old man, wagging his big eyebrows up and down.

True tried to ignore him, to edge off down the street. He'd never wished so hard for his bus before.

"Name's Jackson," the old man said, before coughing and spitting into a handkerchief.

"First name or last name, sir?" True asked, curious in spite of himself.

"Both."

"Both? You just have the one name?"

"Yes, more or less. My name's Jackson M. Jackson. And you're True Monroe. Now I'm talking to you as a friend of Mrs. Douglas's.

Marie has been my friend for years, ever since I sold her that side of this duplex. And what you did to her troubles me greatly, for her sake and yours," said Jackson M. Jackson.

"Mr. Jackson, have you seen Mrs. Douglas?"

"Have I seen her? What exactly do you mean by that?" Mr. Jackson coughed again, this time leaning way over to spit on the sidewalk.

True wondered if Mr. Jackson was sick or if all old men coughed and spit this much. "Have you seen her since . . . the day before yesterday?" True didn't want to ask *have you seen her since I broke into her house?*

"Marie's upset, True. Upset by the damage, by the theft, by the fact it was someone she knew who did this to her. I talked to her last night, and she still couldn't believe you'd have done such a thing."

True finally heard the sound he'd been hoping for, his bus, the driver grinding through the gears. He shifted his backpack with relief. "I have to go to school now," he said.

"True?"

"Yes, Mr. Jackson?"

"You come by on your way home. You need to apologize to Mrs. Douglas, and I want you to think of a way to try to make up for what you've done."

THIRTEEN

APOLOGIZE? Make up for what he'd done? How? What'd he have to run into Mr. Jackson for? True couldn't believe his bad luck. He looked for his friend William on the bus. He was near the back on the left side, his small, shaved head nearly hidden by the other kids around him. William was wearing a Giants football jersey and looked surprised and happy to see him.

"DUUUUDE!" said William, trying to act all that as he slapped True hard on the hand. "Waaasuuup?"

True didn't feel like playing around. He didn't want people to look at him today. Today, he wished he were invisible. Hadn't he had enough trouble to deal with already, with Mr. Jackson?

True could see Wesley just now leaping up the steps to get on the bus right before the doors closed. Usually Wesley rode his bike, but True guessed their mom must have asked Wesley to keep an eye on True while he was at school. So here was Wesley, tagging along behind his little brother as a favor to their mom. True ignored Wesley, but he could feel Wesley look over William before they sat down. Wesley must have decided William was okay because he took a seat toward the front of the bus near some seniors he knew.

William looked at True like he'd been away all summer. "Did you go to jail?" he said. Then when True didn't answer right away, he said, "I didn't think you'd do it, man. Ringo said you would, or else. We heard the glass break and knew you were in, then it seemed like you were gone forever. I saw the police car come up—just your bad luck they were close by—when I ran away, they caught me too."

"What did you tell them?"

"Man, I didn't tell them nothin'." William stopped, took a deep breath.

True said, "Uh, huh," then just sat there and thought about it. With the way William liked to talk, it was very hard to imagine him saying nothing to the police.

William said, "True, Ringo said you in the Club now. You proved yourself. He said I can be too, but I gotta be tested first. I gotta do what he tells me to do."

"What'd he tell you to do, Boy?" asked True. True was thinking about what William had told him about belonging to the Club now. He didn't feel happy like he thought he would. He was filled instead with a cold feeling, with worry about what might come next.

"He didn't say," said William. "He said he'd let me know next time the Club meets. But True," said William as the bus stopped in front of the high school, "he told me to tell you the Club meets tonight, and he expects you to be there. He's going to give you your own jacket."

"Tonight?" asked True. He thought of his promise to his mom to stay away from trouble. Then he thought of the rich smell of the leather jacket Ringo would give him if he told his mom one more lie, snuck out one more time. Was it worth it? True pushed his fists deep into his pockets and touched the gold ring. What should he do?

"True?"

"Yeah?"

"Were you scared? When they carried you off in the police car?"

True knew he should tell Boy the truth, about how he couldn't stop shaking even though the officers had the heat turned way up, how he could taste his own blood in his mouth from his cut lip, how the crackle of the police radio made him jump. True didn't want to admit to Boy how scared he'd been.

"Scared? No," True lied.

FOURTEEN

IT was a long, strange day for True. He was relieved to be back in his regular routine, but it was hard to look people in the eye. True realized he didn't know who knew where he'd been and who didn't. Though it felt like he'd been gone for at least a week, in reality it had only been a day. Beyond the safety of taking notes, changing classes, and grumbling about tests, True now felt there was a whole, lawless world out there that he no longer wanted to be a part of.

True felt better in class. He didn't have any classes with Ringo or Allfire, which was good because he was most nervous about being around them again. Still, when the bell rang and it was time to change classes, True felt his palms grow cold and sweaty and his heart begin to pound. He was relieved each time he made it to his next class without running into anyone else from the Club.

True thought what a relief it would be if he could just change schools and start all over somewhere else where no one would know him. He could be anybody! He could be a jock or class president, not some gangster wanna-be. Is that what this was? A gang?

When True entered his English classroom for his last class of the day, he heard a familiar "Yo, True" and turned to see NoWay looking at him anxiously from his desk right in front of True's. True felt a sinking feeling in his stomach as he slid into his seat.

"True-Blue! You okay, man?" NoWay asked in a low voice. He lightly slapped palms up with True.

"Hey, NoWay. What's up?"

"What's up? You tell me," NoWay said impatiently. "What happened to you after you got caught?"

"What do you think?" True said, glancing around him. He wasn't really angry at NoWay. NoWay wasn't as shrewd as Ringo or quite as mean as Allfire. It's just that True didn't really want to talk about this at school. He remembered his detention and knew there might not be a better time to talk with NoWay.

So True sighed and said quietly, "They took me to the Youth Study Center. I'm only home under detention. If I go anywhere except school, they'll pick me up again and slap me in some group home. It ain't good, NoWay. I still got a hearing to decide if the judge finds me guilty or not, then another one after that to tell me my punishment if he finds me guilty. And he's going to find me guilty, NoWay. They caught me loaded up with that lady's stuff."

True leaned back, his eyes lingering on NoWay's leather jacket. What had NoWay done to "earn" his jacket? I'm not sure it's all worth it, thought True, but he said, "NoWay, what happened yesterday while I was gone?"

NoWay started to tell him about what the teacher had covered in *Middlemarch*, the English novel by George Eliot their teacher was trying to convince them was worth their time and effort. "That chick Dorothea is actually going to marry slimeball Casaubon, but I think Will Ladislaw is more her type," NoWay whispered as the tardy bell rang and the class grew quieter to copy the teacher's chalky notes from the board.

"I didn't mean in the book, NoWay! I meant, did anything happen with the Club?" True whispered.

"Oh, after you got picked up?" said NoWay. "Well . . ." But the teacher, frowning at them, began to lecture.

"There's a meeting tonight, True," whispered

NoWay, and True was glad he didn't have time to answer.

After class, as True walked to his bus with NoWay telling him more about *Middlemarch*, True thought what a good teacher NoWay would be. He really liked books. True was feeling relieved. He'd made it through the day without having to talk with Ringo, who was bound to be disappointed in him for getting caught, for not getting away with anything. Well, thought True guiltily, *almost nothing*, as his hand squeezed Mrs. Douglas's warm gold ring in his jeans pocket. NoWay turned to go, and True was just winging up onto the first step of the bus when he heard Ringo call, "Truuue!"

True turned and looked down. Ringo was standing there, squinting up at him, sun in his eyes. He had on a Hilfiger jersey and baggy trousers. He looked happy to see True.

"True! Where you been all day, brother?"

"Around," said True.

"Boy told you, right? Meeting tonight? Be there," said Ringo, turning to go.

"I would—I mean—I can't," said True, turning back up the stairs to go into the bus as a couple of other kids were waiting to get on. But Ringo grabbed his sleeve and pulled him back down.

Eye to eye, Ringo said pleasantly, "What do you mean, you can't?" True could see NoWay looking uncomfortable behind Ringo, but he didn't say or do anything to stop him.

"I've got detention, Ringo. If I break it, the judge will lock me up somewhere else, and—"

Wesley appeared behind Ringo, pulled Ringo back away from True, then pushed Ringo roughly on his shoulder. "He said he can't come to your little meeting, and that's going to have to be enough for you," said Wesley, pushing his glasses back up onto his nose.

Wesley might not be a natural fighter, but True thought Ringo couldn't know that from looking at him right now. Wesley had a dangerous glint in his eyes that seemed to say "anyone messes with my little brother, messes with me," and Ringo saw it too.

"Wha—who are you, man? What business is it of yours?" Ringo asked, but he backed off.

"I'm his brother. You need to leave him alone now. He doesn't hang with you anymore. Get on the bus, True," said Wesley, and True did what he was told for once. Behind him, he imagined Ringo staring after them as they rode off on the bus. True was grateful for Wesley in a way he never had been before. He couldn't remember Wesley—or anyone else—ever saving him from anything like that.

"Wesley?" said True.

Wesley was sitting in the seat across from him. He turned toward True.

"Thanks."

"Okay. Now you've got to do your part. Stay away from him, True. That kid is trouble. I've seen him around before, and you are messing with fire."

True leaned his forehead against the glass of the window. Wesley seemed so sure. True felt like he'd let everyone down—his mom, Wesley, and Ringo too. What could he do to prove himself to Ringo but get free from him as well? One thing was for sure, he did not want to get caught breaking his detention rules. He didn't want to have to leave home to go live in some group home with a bunch of strangers. True decided he would not try to sneak out tonight for the meeting, no matter how threatening Ringo was. What could Ringo do about it, anyway?

FIFTEEN

WALKING home, True remembered Mr. Jackson's words from this morning. He knew he'd have to see Mrs. Douglas sooner or later. Wesley waited for True on the sidewalk while True walked up the steps and knocked on Mr. Jackson's storm door. It was a chilly afternoon, and True felt the sun disappear behind a cloud. Jackson M. Jackson looked surprised to see him. His fuzzy caterpillar eyebrows shot up onto his forehead.

"You! Well, well. I guess it's too soon to give up on today's youth after all," he said as he struggled to free the lock on the storm door. As True stepped back, the door banged open against the wall. Mr. Jackson stepped out in a rumpled blue cardigan sweater, gray plaid trousers, and house slippers.

"Let's just see if Mrs. Douglas is available," he said. As True and Wesley followed behind him the few steps over to Mrs. Douglas's door, True wondered if Mr. Jackson wore those slippers all day. Seemed like he'd be embarrassed for everyone to see them.

Mr. Jackson nodded at Wesley. "That your brother?" he stated, not really asking the question. "You take after each other. He better behaved than you?"

True nodded, then looked away. Mr. Jackson knocked. After a few minutes, True could see Mrs. Douglas peering at them through the storm door. She opened it and stood there looking at them.

"Mrs. Douglas? Mr. Jackson felt it was only right, because of what happened . . . I mean, what I did, that I . . ." True couldn't get the words out. He looked at his shoes, then at Mr. Jackson's slippers. Finally, he looked up at Mrs. Douglas and saw to his surprise and horror that she was crying.

"True, I've known you since you were just a baby. If you were a little smaller and I were a little younger, I'd be tempted to paddle you."

"Mrs. Douglas, I'm sorry. I didn't think. I wish I'd never done it," True said. And he meant it.

Mrs. Douglas leaned on the door frame and wiped her cheeks with a handkerchief she pulled from the pocket of her housedress. She blew her nose and continued to talk as though she hadn't heard True. "My daughter Rosie's in California. She's worried about me. Doesn't think I should live alone here anymore. She says this proves it isn't safe."

"Now, that Rosie, she's a worrier," Mr. Jackson chimed in before a coughing attack kept him busy for the next minute or so.

"Well, that's so, but maybe she's got good cause to worry," said Mrs. Douglas. "She's talking 'bout she wants me to move out to San Diego where I'd be close to her and my grandbabies."

Mr. Jackson looked distressed. "San Diego? Why, that's practically in Mexico! You don't want to go live in the desert, now do you?"

Mrs. Douglas smiled. "It's a long way from here. But she may be right. I don't know if I am safe anymore or if I can keep up with this house. How am I going to get my storm door down this year or get my flowers in the ground? And I still have that back window to replace," she said, looking at True. "Maybe I'm getting too old for this. Maybe Rosie's right."

"Mrs. Douglas, I could help you with the storm door, and True here could help you in the garden. True should pay to have that glass replaced in the back, anyway," said Wesley. True was surprised. It was a good idea to help

Mrs. Douglas so she could stay, but what did Wesley have to go and say he'd pay for that window for? There went his new FUBU shoes.

"Yes, we could help you out," said True doubtfully.

"You? Well, I'll think about it," said Mrs. Douglas skeptically as she eyed True with a mixture of fear and pity.

"I hope you'll say yes, Marie. I think the boys are sincere. The work will be good medicine for True, and it might convince Rosie that you're okay here," Mr. Jackson said.

Wesley and True went home. True was glad to get there. "TGIF," said Wesley, spinning the front tire of his bike as he sat on it in their room, pretending to pop a wheelie. True threw himself down on his bed and watched the wheel spinning in air. He wondered if Mrs. Douglas would have to move away. Both she and Mr. Jackson were very upset at the idea. It was all True's fault too. He never thought he'd get caught or of all the trouble it would cause. Would he be able to make up for what he'd done?

SIXTEEN

SATURDAY True had a visit from his caseworker. True's mom was nervous about the visit. True, Wesley, and their mother had vacuumed, mopped, and dusted Friday night so the house would be clean and tidy. The caseworker was not intimidating after all. He turned out to be a thin, young white man who looked like he wasn't much older than Wesley. He wore a cheap blue dress shirt with a button-down collar and a wide necktie that looked like a brown and gold checkerboard. He had watery blue eyes and very pale skin, as though he never went outside except to get into his car.

The caseworker introduced himself as Jeff Payne. He sat down on the sofa next to True. True's mother sat on a chair across the coffee table, while Wesley disappeared to his room. True wished he could go upstairs too. He felt silly and stiff.

"How are things going, Ms. Monroe? Has True been following the rules set by the judge for his detention?" asked Mr. Payne.

"Good, good," said True's mom, "True's been doing very well. Can I get you some coffee?" she asked.

"No, thank you," said Mr. Payne. True thought of all his mom's work preparing fresh coffee and finding a sugar bowl in the kitchen cabinets to wash and fill. If she was disappointed, she didn't show it.

"And how about for you, True? How was school yesterday?"

"It was fine," said True. Then he remembered the incident with Ringo and wondered if he should mention it. It didn't seem that important right now.

Mr. Payne leaned forward. "Ms. Monroe, we need to talk about the next hearing. If True is not going to enter a plea, it will be another few months before he has his judiciary hearing. If you are planning to enter a guilty plea, then we can get a hearing a week from Monday. It's up to you, Ms. Monroe."

Mr. Payne didn't seem to believe in small talk. True's mom looked at True, then at Mr. Payne. "Mr. Payne, I know some parents will pretend their children never do wrong. But my son did something wrong. And I believe the only way True is going to get his life straightened out is by being honest about that. So we ought to go ahead and enter a guilty plea so we can get on with the business of living."

"I respect your decision, Ms. Monroe. I don't need to come back now until Monday. By then I hope we will know if the court date is set. Meanwhile, True, you know to keep abiding by the rules of your detention, right?"

"Yes, sir," said True.

"Would it be all right for True to go to church with us tomorrow? Then straight on home, of course," asked Ms. Monroe.

"That would be fine. See you on Monday," said Mr. Payne as he hurried out to his car.

True felt nervous about having the next hearing in a week. He didn't ever want to go back to the Youth Study Center, even for just an hour or two. He didn't want to see the judge again or answer his questions. But he knew he had to, so he might as well just get it over with as soon as possible.

SEVENTEEN

IN Germantown, you knew when it was Sunday. Every other day the streets were packed with people on foot shopping, standing in long lines at the bank, grocery store, or check-cashing windows, and people in cars double-parking, parallel parking, yelling, and honking their car horns. On Sunday, all the stores on Chelten Avenue stayed closed, with their metal gates pulled down over the doorways and locked up tight. Beer and soda bottles, chip bags, hot dog wrappers, and other assorted trash lay on the sidewalks and in the gutters from Saturday night's party crowd. The check-cashing windows were closed, and so were the pawnshops, thrift shops, video parlors, and shoe shops.

The streets were nearly deserted as True, Wesley, and their mom walked to church, but people they passed were also all dressed up for worship. It was mild and sunny, but still cold enough to wear heavy coats. The Monroes weren't regular churchgoers, though they belonged to a local congregation. When True's mom was depressed, she didn't go anywhere, including church. Once they fell out of the habit of attending, it was hard to go back. True's mom worried what people would think of them.

The church was a solid stone building set back from the houses near the street on a corner lot. To get into the sanctuary, they had to walk through a stone archway, which led into a quiet and peaceful courtyard. The courtyard had a small lawn, flower beds, a few trees, three stone benches, and a worn stone cross with one crumbling arm. A previous pastor had brought the cross back from a trip to the Holy Land. It was colder in the courtyard than it was on the street because the sun had not yet penetrated the shade. True would have liked to stay there, out in the courtyard. It felt safe, like nothing bad could happen to him there.

The sermon was on Jesus's baptism in the river Jordan. The pastor said it was about Jesus and his relationship with his father. "See how God says to Jesus, 'You are my beloved son, with you I am well pleased?' Can you imagine that? A God who's well pleased with you? Do you know when God sees you coming, God comes running out to meet you? God loves us, people.

Isaiah 43:1 says, 'Do not fear for I have redeemed you; I have called you by name, you are mine. God is love.' Now, we are going in to the hard work of Lent. Life ain't always easy, amen! I want you to remember when you are down, when you think you can't get it right, that God is right there, loving you. Let's work on laying hold of this and claiming it for ourselves this week. Amen! Amen."

During the coffee hour after church, Pastor Williams talked with Ms. Monroe while Wesley and True waited for her. They stood around in the fellowship hall, drinking punch and eating store-bought sugar cookies. On the way home, their mom was excited. She was walking much faster than she had walked to church.

"What did you and Pastor Williams talk about, Mom?" asked True. He was worried they had been talking about him and that the pastor might have given his mother some big ideas.

"I told him about how I am looking for a new job and about maybe taking some nursing classes. He wants me to stop in to schedule a meeting with their job counselor. She's new— just started a couple of months ago, but he said she's really good and the service is free. She might know of some good job leads for me."

True and Wesley noticed their mom's good

mood seemed to last the rest of the day. It was nice, and weird, to listen to her downstairs as she hummed hymns and banged pots around cooking Sunday dinner. Just like a regular family, thought True, as he lay on his bed reading *Middlemarch*.

He was reading the chapter "Old and Young" and came to the part in which Mr. Vincy is defending his son Fred to Mr. Bulstrode, the banker, by saying, "He is not a liar. I don't want to make him better than he is. . . . But he is not a liar. And I should have thought—but I may be wrong—that there was no religion to hinder a man from believing the best of a young fellow, when you don't know worse."

True thought to himself, I have been a liar, but I don't have to keep on being one.

"True! Wesley! Supper!" called their mom. *Weather report—a sunny day.*

EIGHTEEN

MONDAY morning, Boy wasn't on the bus. Wesley wasn't either—he'd gone back to riding his bike. True rode to school by himself, trying to decide what to do with the ring he'd been carrying around in his pocket. Holding on to it wasn't helping him any—he knew he needed to do something with it.

At school True kept expecting to run into Ringo. All day, True kept watching for him because he didn't want to find Ringo suddenly standing behind him. Ringo was bound to be angry that True hadn't gone to his meeting Friday night. Ringo was sure to be embarrassed about Wesley making him back down in front of True and NoWay by the bus Friday afternoon too. Ringo hadn't been angry at True before. True didn't like the idea of having Ringo for an enemy.

Before English class, True waited for NoWay to show up. Finally he did, just before the bell, looking upset. He was carrying a load of papers, books, and pens, and he kept dropping papers.

"Hey, NoWay," True said.

NoWay said, "Hey," but didn't look at him as he sat down.

"Come on, man, don't act like that. I couldn't help it. I couldn't go to the meeting. I had no choice."

"Look, True, about that meeting—I want you to know I had nothing to do with it, okay? It wasn't my idea, and I didn't help."

"Nothing to do with what? What are you talking about, NoWay?"

"You'll see," said NoWay, and the bell rang.

After school True was getting his geometry book from his locker when he heard someone running down the hall toward him. "True!"

It was Wesley. True had never seen Wesley look so bad. He was crying and looked disoriented. It was like someone had shaken him upside down until his teeth rattled, then dropped him on his head. "True, True, True . . . Come with me, you gotta see what they did, I can't believe it. Those guys are losers. Losers!"

Wesley pulled True along down the hall and outside. A bunch of people stood around looking at something, but they moved aside to let Wesley and True get through. It was Wesley's bike. The beautiful, sleek, yellow and blue Trek was still locked to the bike rack, but it looked like it had been hit by a load of bricks. The tires were slashed. One fender was bent up and pointed off to the left at an odd angle. The frame was bent and dented. The whole thing was somehow wrapped back around the bike rack.

True was in shock. "Wesley, I . . . I can't believe this. I am so sorry. This is all my—"

"No, it's not. It's not your fault, so don't say that. You know whose fault it is, don't take the blame for him. True, it took me a whole summer to save enough for this bike. What am I gonna do?"

True remembered what NoWay had said about how he had nothing to do with what was going to happen. True began to feel a heat rising inside him from his stomach. He touched Wesley's shoulder and said, "Wesley, I'm going to call Mom and see if she's home. Maybe she can come and help us get your bike home."

Wesley was just staring helplessly at it.

"It looks like somebody took a sledgehammer to it," one girl observed. "Who'd want to do that to you?"

Wesley looked at True. "Remember what I told you, True. That punk is not your friend."

NINETEEN

TRUE reported the damage to the principal's office, then called their mom, who had just gotten in from work. She said she would come right over. On his way back to help Wesley, True saw NoWay walking off down the street. He ran to catch up with him.

NoWay was surprised. "I thought you'd gone," he said.

"NoWay, tell me what happened to Wesley's bike."

"Aw, man, you know what happened. Ringo was so mad at Wesley for making him look bad on Friday, he decided to teach him a lesson."

"So he smashed his bike up," said True.

"You mean he had it done. You know he never does anything himself," said NoWay.

"Who did it?" asked True.

"Like I told you True, it wasn't me. I—"

"Come on, NoWay. Maybe you didn't actually hit the bike, but you knew about it, and you could have stopped it."

"Allfire did it and looked like he enjoyed himself too. Look, True, I'm sorry I didn't do anything about Wesley's bike. I didn't know what this was going to be like. I don't want to be a part of it anymore."

"I got to go. My mom is on her way, and if she sees me here talking to you, I'll be in even more trouble." True walked back to the bike. By now everyone was gone except Wesley, who had managed to unlock it and was trying to bend back the frame.

Their mom was frightened by the incident. After they put the mangled bike into the trunk of the Metro and tied the hatch down with twine, she drove them home. She kept glancing over at Wesley and peering at True in the rearview mirror. "What do you know about this, boys?"

They told her what they knew. When they got home, they saw Mr. Payne just scurrying from his car to their front door. "Oh, hello! I've been waiting for you in my car. I was just about to leave you a note," he said, holding up a scrap of paper.

When they'd managed to carry the bike around to the back of the house, they went inside together. Ms. Monroe made coffee, and this time Mr. Payne accepted a cup while

Wesley and True told him what had happened.

"Unfortunately, it's not surprising. They are trying to scare you into backing down. Just keep away from them while this plays itself out," said Mr. Payne encouragingly.

Easy for him to say, thought True, I *have* been staying away from them.

Mr. Payne told them he had a bit of good news to share. The judiciary court date was set for next Tuesday morning. "I entered your plea, and that helped to speed things up. I know you'll be glad to have that over with."

After Mr. Payne left, True went out back to check on Wesley, who was making minor adjustments with his tool kit on the twisted bike. It was clear to True that the bike was not fixable. "Wesley, if I have any money left after I pay Mrs. Douglas back for the glass I broke, I'm going to help you start saving for a new bike."

Wesley looked up and managed a weak smile. "Thanks, True, but it will take a while to save enough again to replace this bike."

True sat on the peeling back steps and thought about what Mr. Payne had said. *Just stay away from them while this plays itself out*, he'd said. It sounded like a good plan. But how could True keep Ringo away from him?

TWENTY

TUESDAY, Wesley rode the bus with True. Boy wasn't on it. True didn't see Boy, Allfire, or Ringo all day. Before English class, NoWay asked True if he'd thought about how to get out of the Club. "I'm afraid Ringo will beat the pulp out of me, you know?"

True could understand how NoWay felt, though it seemed weird for a big guy like NoWay to worry about getting beaten up by a small guy like Ringo. Ringo just happened to be twice as mean.

By Wednesday, True wanted to see Ringo. He hadn't seen him since last Friday, and he was sick of tiptoeing around school, scared of his own shadow. Wednesday morning, Boy was on the bus. Wesley sat up front with a friend, and True went to sit with Boy. Boy seemed embarrassed to see True.

"Where you been?" True asked, as he sat down beside Boy. "Oh, you know . . ." said Boy vaguely, and he shrugged.

"So you know about Wesley's bike," said True. "Did you help them?"

Boy held up his hands. "No, no I didn't. Look, I'm sorry 'bout that, seeing as how it's your brother and all, but I guess he had it coming."

"Had it coming! William, do you really believe that?"

Boy shrugged again and looked out the window. For a few minutes, they rode in silence. Then True said, "You know, even if you didn't have anything to do with the bike, sooner or later it will be your turn. Ringo's going to want you to prove yourself. You need to watch out for him." Boy looked at True with something like surprise, or worry.

"True?"

"Yeah?"

"Don't tell anybody this. I can trust you, right?"

"Yeah," True said, wary.

"You're right. Ringo wants me to earn my jacket. He wants me to help him steal a car."

"William, it's a bad idea. He's just using you. He doesn't care about you, and he won't care if you get caught. Believe me, I know. You think Ringo cares I got arrested?"

"You made the mistake of getting caught. I

just won't get caught, that's all. Just think, if I just do this one little thing, then I'm in!" Boy's face was joyful, just thinking about it.

"I can't even talk to you anymore. What happened to you? I thought you were my friend," True said, as the bus lurched to a halt. True got up and lined up to get off. "Thought you had more sense than that," True said.

Boy rolled his eyes. "You screwed up, True! Maybe you just ain't Club material!"

"I have nothing left to say to you, fool," True said as he walked off the bus.

After lunch as True opened the door to leave the restroom, he bumped right into Ringo, who was on his way in. Ringo smiled. "Long time no see, True-Blue." He made it sound like True had been away on vacation. "Too bad about your brother's bike, man."

True stared at him. "Why'd you do that? What did it prove?"

Ringo took True's arm and pulled him over to the side of the door to let a guy get past. "He brought that down on himself, True. Bad karma, man. Some people just have to be taught respect. They just not naturally respectful. Not you, True. You different." He leaned closer to True, as though to tell him a secret. True felt like jerking his head away and had to force himself to hold still. "Now you know how it is. If you still in the Club, you need to prove it. I got a little job planned with you and Boy. You still on my team, right?" Ringo locked his elbow around True's head in a mock wrestling hold. True broke free, and shoved Ringo on the arm.

True wanted Ringo to leave him alone. "Look, Ringo," said True, "I—"

"So True," sang Ringo softly, "you are so True, aren't you?" he said, shadowboxing True's arm. The late bell rang for class, and True realized he and Ringo were alone in the bathroom. "You're a free man, True," said Ringo. "You didn't let them scare you, right? You're still in, right?" His light brown eyes narrowed as he stared at True.

"Ringo, I don't want to be in your Club anymore." True started for the door.

Ringo grabbed his shirt and shoved him against the wall. "What did you say?" Ringo held on to him.

But True wouldn't back down. "You can't make me steal a car for you, man. I don't have to."

Ringo hit True hard in his stomach. True crumpled up and fell on the ground. It hurt bad, and True's eyes were closed around the pain. Ringo got right down next to True. "Wrong answer, man. I am so disappointed in you, True. How could you do this to me after all I've done for you? All the money I spent on you, stuff I bought for you. It's like you stabbing me in the back. I ought to turn you in to the cops for delivering that stolen stuff. You act like you all righteous. You owe me, man."

True opened his eyes and slowly stood up. He thought he might be sick at first, then the feeling passed. As he straightened out his clothes, he remembered the ring in his pocket. No one knew he had it. If he gave it away, no one would ever know. True reached in his left pocket and pulled out Mrs. Douglas's gold ring. It was warm and heavy in his palm. "Here, Ringo. We're even. I don't owe you nothing."

If True thought Ringo was going to be pleased with the ring, he was wrong. Ringo took it and examined it. Then he looked at True with an ugly, greedy look on his face.

"You been holding out on me, True? Where'd this come from? The old lady's house?"

"Yeah, Ringo. Now that's it, you've been paid in full and then some for any money you spent on me. Leave me alone." True turned to go.

Ringo's words stopped him. "Maybe I'll go back and break into her house again myself. I bet there's more where this came from. And if I can't find it, I'll make the old lady tell me."

A chill ran through True. He knew Ringo might really do it. True was scared at just the thought of Ringo letting himself in to Mrs. Douglas's house. He could picture him threatening the old lady and knew she'd have nothing to give him to satisfy his desire for money.

"What do you want from me?" True asked, his back to Ringo.

Ringo said, "That's more like it. Make one more delivery for me. Tomorrow night at midnight."

True thought of the risk. He'd have to sneak out of his house, go to Paradise Towers alone, and over to the drop-off point. If he was caught, he wouldn't be going home again. Fear rose in him, then Mrs. Douglas's face appeared in his mind, the soft lines creasing into a smile.

"Okay. One last time," True said.

TWENTY-ONE

TRUE thought Thursday would never end. The minutes dragged by. He wanted the day, the whole day, to be over. He wanted the delivery to be over and to be home safe again in his bed, free of Ringo. He wanted Mrs. Douglas to be safe. The more he thought about giving Ringo the ring, the worse he felt. He had thought it would make Ringo happy. It had only made him angry and more threatening than ever. But as soon as this was over, he'd finally be free of the Club.

First, though, he had to endure the regular day and the regular meeting with his mother and Mr. Payne, who were proud of him for doing so well. "See that, True? Things are all working themselves out," said Mr. Payne as he nodded approvingly. "Come Tuesday, you'll have your hearing and be able to move on."

True wanted to believe this was so. Right now, Tuesday seemed to be a long way off.

Then supper, dishes, homework, showers.

Ms. Monroe went to bed at 10:00. True put on his sweatshirt and sweatpants, got in bed, and turned off his light at 10:30. Then he waited for Wesley to go to sleep too. It seemed as if Wesley was going to read all night. Finally at 11:00, he turned off his light. The house was dark and quiet.

True waited until, by the green glow of the tiny light on his digital watch, he saw it was 11:40. He got out of bed, quietly picked up his sneakers, and left the bedroom. He pulled the door closed soundlessly behind him. The house was very dark, but by the hall nightlight True went downstairs, stepping on the outer edges of the stairs so they squeaked less and avoiding the second one from the bottom altogether because it always creaked. True put on his shoes, a ski cap, and his heavy jacket. He unbolted the door, slid the chain off, and opened it. The storm door squeaked in protest, and a dog started to bark somewhere down the street. True closed the door behind him as quietly as he could, then started off down the street. The sky was overcast, and it was raining lightly.

At first True thought, it's just my luck that it would rain. But then after he walked for a few minutes, he thought it might be a good thing, after all. He knew it was dangerous to be out alone after dark, and especially this late at night. The rain might keep people inside and help to keep him safe.

It was spooky to have to walk up the stairs of Paradise Towers alone, at midnight. Around every corner, True imagined someone was waiting to jump him. He was cold and wet from the light, but steady, rain. What floor did Ringo live on again? Was it the fourth? True started to go down the hall of the fourth floor. He saw shadows moving ahead and froze. He heard the sound of a man's low voice and a woman laughing. They were leaning against each other by a door ahead. True walked quietly back to the stairs. This wasn't right. It was the next floor.

True went up to Ringo's door and waited. Should he knock? What if Ringo's parents answered? What would he say? True waited, the cold settling in around him, his right hand aching. The cold made it hurt. After a minute, he knocked softly. Ringo opened it. He was still dressed, and the lights were all on inside. True blinked as his eyes adjusted to the glare.

"Good. I knew you wouldn't let me down," Ringo said with a smile. "You don't want me to pay Grandma a visit, do you? Wait here," he said, without waiting for an answer.

The Club

True stood by the half-opened door. The heat that poured out felt good. The TV blared a late-night comic's stand-up routine. Seemed like every light in the place was on. When Ringo came back with an envelope, True said, "You alone?" He thought Ringo would have to sneak out to give him the envelope, but Ringo was clearly not worried about getting caught.

"Yeah. I'm alone. Now take this to the same place as last time, the barbershop on Wayne. Give it to the same guy."

"Do I have to say anything?"

"Not if you recognize him. If you ain't sure, same words as last time. 'It's True,' then he'll say 'it's not.'"

True stuffed the bulky envelope inside his jacket. He turned to go.

"True—here. Last chance, man." True looked, and saw Ringo was offering him a beautiful black leather jacket. True touched it. "Go on, try it on."

True could smell the rich scent of the leather. He imagined the silky lining, the weight of it on his shoulders.

"No, thanks, Ringo. It's not my style." True turned and walked away.

TWENTY-TWO

TRUE made his way back down the stairs. The rain was heavier now. It felt like winter again. The corners of the manila envelope poked True in the chest and stomach. As he walked along, he put his hands in the pockets of his jacket and held the envelope still. The rain was keeping the streets quiet, but a couple of cars passed True as he walked. One slowed down as it passed him. True hurried up, trying not to look. The car peeled out, splashing him. True turned down his street to get away from the car, in case it came back. He slowed at the empty lot, and without thinking, turned in to it.

It was muddy, and the trash bags, tires, and old mattress were threatening shadows. Every corner looked like a place some creep was waiting with a gun. True breathed hard. The cold air stung his chest. He had to know what he was carrying this time. He crouched down by the wall and took out the envelope. He carefully tore open the flap with his stiff fingers and dumped the contents into his lap. By the flickering orange glow of a streetlight, True saw a tangle of gold necklaces around a large, dull black gun. There were some small plastic tubes with crystals in them. A gun! It could have been used to kill somebody! Ringo was using him to carry drugs and a gun! Crap. And Mrs. Douglas's ring. He held the ring up. Here it was again. Like he had been given another chance.

Crap. True tried to steady himself as he took a deep breath. What should he do? If his father were here, what would he tell him to do? True was filled with a longing for his father, for someone to guide him. Suddenly, True saw Mr. Jackson's face in his mind the day Mr. Jackson defended him to Mrs. Douglas. He said it was too soon to give up on today's youth. True thought of the kind look Mr. Jackson had given him after he had apologized to Mrs. Douglas. He'd know what to do. True put everything back in the envelope and zipped the envelope up in his jacket. He walked down to Mr. Jackson's house and knocked on the door. He had to ring the doorbell a few times and wait a while before Mr. Jackson showed up at the door in his pajamas and robe. He didn't look too surprised to see True. "Come in, you okay there? Wipe your feet on the mat." True did as he was told.

He went into the warmth of Mr. Jackson's musty living room and waited while Mr. Jackson turned on a lamp. He gave Mr. Jackson the envelope and told him everything. "It was Mrs. Douglas, sir. I only said yes because I was afraid Ringo would hurt her." Mr. Jackson nodded and asked him to wait while he called the police.

"If you are quick about it, by golly, you can catch the fellow waiting for the goods and the fellow waiting for the payoff!" said Mr. Jackson into the phone. "True here can help. He'll be here waiting. You best hurry though, or they'll get suspicious."

A police squad car was in the area and only took a minute to arrive. Mr. Jackson told them his plan: True would go on to deliver the stolen goods, and the police could arrest the guy who takes them after he gives True the money. Then they could follow True back to Paradise Towers and arrest Ringo when he takes the money from True. The officers talked and agreed, calling for backup.

True was exhausted and cold. He didn't want to go back out there to face Ringo again. Hadn't he done enough? Mr. Jackson must have read True's feelings on his face because he turned to True and said gently, "True, this is your chance to make a real difference. I don't blame you if you don't want to do it. I understand. But if you help, we could get to the bottom of all the break-ins going on. You up for it, son?"

Son. True looked into Mr. Jackson's kind, rough face. "Okay. What do I need to do?"

The first part went smoothly, without a hitch. The two police officers followed True—one in the car with the lights off and one on foot—to the barbershop. The police car stopped out of sight. The tall, thin guy was lounging in the shadows by the barbershop door. "It's True," True whispered. "It's not," the man hissed back. True handed off the envelope with trembling hands. He hated to let go of Mrs. Douglas's ring again. The man took it and handed True a smaller envelope, like he had the time before. Once again, the tall man faded back into the shadows and began to disappear behind the barbershop. Only this time, the policeman on foot who'd watched the whole thing caught him and called for his partner on his radio. They cuffed the man, who struggled and cursed.

Then it was back to Paradise Towers. "We'd give you a ride, bud, but that would give you away," said one of the officers.

He was tall, muscular, and medium brown. He looked kind, and when True said, "That's okay, thanks anyway," the officer said, "It will all be over soon. You're doing great."

True went back down the street alone. It helped to know the police car was back there following him, but he was still shaking and had to keep his hands pressed hard in his jacket pockets. The rain had stopped. What time was it? True knew he could look to see, but he wanted to try to warm his hands. It felt like hours since he'd crept from his bed. He hoped his mom and Wesley were still asleep, and he was both reassured and sad to see that the house was dark as he went by.

Back to the dark, ugly skeleton of Paradise Towers. A dark blue, unmarked police car was already waiting. True made his way up the stairs, followed by two police officers.

All was quiet on the fifth floor. True knocked on Ringo's door. After a minute, Ringo opened it cautiously. "What took you so long!"

True tried to sound annoyed. "Your friend wasn't there at first to take the delivery. I had to wait for him. Here—" True handed Ringo the envelope with the money.

Ringo took it and opened the door some more. "Thanks, True. Now I've got a little something for you." Ringo opened the door the rest of the way. Allfire was behind the door. He grabbed True and dragged him in. True fell on the floor. Allfire and Ringo began to punch and kick him. It was all True could do to cover his head with his arms to protect his face.

"Stop! Police!" said one of the officers as he pushed open the door.

TWENTY-THREE

EVEN though it had only been three weeks since the night of Ringo and Allfire's arrests, it felt to True like months. True rested his hands on Mrs. Douglas's shovel. It was a beautiful Saturday afternoon. True, Wesley, NoWay, and Boy had spent the last two Saturdays working at Mrs. Douglas's house. True's side ached from his sore ribs, but he looked around the garden with pride. The weeds and litter were gone. He and Boy had worked together to clear away the weeds and turn the earth in the flowerbeds. Now Boy was planting the last few pansies from the flats they'd bought. Boy had never worked in a garden, but after Ringo's arrest, he wanted to make up with True. So when True asked, he'd agreed to help out.

NoWay and Wesley had spent the morning scraping old paint from the back steps and hammering loose boards back into place. Now they were touching up a second coat of dark green paint on the steps. The new kitchen window gleamed from behind a black iron grate they'd installed over the glass, to prevent someone from breaking in that way again. True sighed. It looked so nice that it was a shame Mrs. Douglas would not be staying.

Just then Mrs. Douglas and Mr. Jackson opened the back door and stepped out. "How's it coming, boys?" asked Mr. Jackson.

True smiled. "Just about done, Mr. Jackson. Does it look all right, Mrs. Douglas? I was just thinking you might change your mind and stay."

Mrs. Douglas shook her head. "Well, I'd like to, True, but Rosie is right. I really will be happier being close to her and my grandchildren. And you can't beat the weather in San Diego. I'll miss it here, though. I never thought I'd move. Anyway, I thank you all for your hard work." Mrs. Douglas looked down and stroked the heavy gold ring that was back on her left hand. "True, I'll see you next Saturday, if I don't see you sooner."

Mr. Jackson didn't say anything. He just blew his nose and rubbed at a spot on his shirt. He looked as if he didn't know what to say.

When Mrs. Douglas had gone back in with Mr. Jackson, True thought about how even getting everyone to help fix things for Mrs. Douglas had not erased the harm he'd done by breaking in. If he hadn't broken in, she wouldn't be moving away, and Mr. Jackson wouldn't be losing a good friend and neighbor.

NoWay had been gathering paint stirring sticks and brushes in a pan to wash up. He looked at True. "Well True, how does it feel to have your hearings behind you? And some of this work . . ." With that, NoWay sloshed the paintbrushes in soapy water.

"Really, really good, man." True thought about how lucky he was. The judiciary and sentencing hearings had been combined since True entered a guilty plea. Thanks to Mrs. Douglas and Mr. Jackson testifying for him, Judge Caroset gave True probation. He told True he would be expected to perform restitution—by using six Saturdays to help Mrs. Douglas repair her window, clean up her yard, and whatever else she needed him to do around her house.

Boy moaned and disgustedly tried to wipe the dirt from his hands. "Man. This sucks."

"Just be glad you didn't go with Ringo," said True.

"What, have you heard something?" asked Boy.

"Yeah," True said. "Mr. Payne told me that Ringo's still in that group home waiting for his hearing, but Allfire got in a fight with a kid in his group home and got sent to some juvenile prison."

"Prison!" said Boy.

"Not for good, but if he keeps fighting, I don't guess any placements will take him."

"Some friends they turned out to be," muttered NoWay. He poured out the dirty water into the grass by the chain-link fence and rinsed the brushes again from the hose before laying them out to dry.

True took as deep a breath as he dared to, with the ache in his side. He looked around the muddy garden. It wasn't a garden you'd pick for a magazine cover, but at least you could tell it was a garden.

He thought about how he had felt that night he broke in, how much he thought he had to prove to have true friends. He looked at Boy, NoWay, and Wesley as they gathered up their jackets and supplies. Not everything he'd learned about himself in the past weeks was good news. But True knew that he'd found out who his friends really were. And that was something some people spend a lifetime looking to find out.

"I have ten dollars left," True said. "Let's go down to WaWa and get a couple of subs. I'm starved."